BY MARGARET ATWOOD

FICTION

The Edible Woman
Surfacing
Lady Oracle
Dancing Girls (stories)
Life Before Man
Bodily Harm

POETRY

Selected Poems
The Circle Game
The Animals in That Country
The Journals of Susanna Moodie
Procedures for Underground
Power Politics
You Are Happy
Two-Headed Poems

CRITICISM

Survival: A Thematic Guide to Canadian Literature

TRUE STORIES

Margaret Atwood

SIMON AND SCHUSTER
NEW YORK

Copyright © Margaret Atwood 1981
All rights reserved
including the right of reproduction
in whole or in part in any form
Published by Simon and Schuster
A Division of Gulf & Western Corporation
Simon & Schuster Building
Rockefeller Center
1230 Avenue of the Americas
New York, New York 10020
Originally published in Canada
by Oxford University Press
SIMON AND SCHUSTER and colophon
are trademarks of Simon & Schuster
Manufactured in the United States of America

10   9   8   7   6   5   4   3   2   1

Library of Congress Cataloging in Publication Data

Atwood, Margaret Eleanor, date.
   True stories.

   Reprint. Originally published: Toronto: Oxford
University Press, 1981.
   I. Title.
PR9199.3.A8T7   1982   811'.54   82-5456
ISBN 0-671-45271-1   AACR2
ISBN 0-671-45971-6 PBK

CONTENTS

TRUE STORIES

i

Don't ask for the true story;
why do you need it?

It's not what I set out with
or what I carry.

What I'm sailing with,
a knife, blue fire,

luck, a few good words
that still work, and the tide.

ii

The true story was lost
on the way down to the beach, it's something

I never had, that black tangle
of branches in a shifting light,

my blurred footprints
filling with salt

water, this handful
of tiny bones, this owl's kill;

a moon, crumpled papers, a coin,
the glint of an old picnic,

the hollows made by lovers
in sand a hundred

years ago: no clue.

iii

The true story lies
among the other stories,

a mess of colours, like jumbled clothing
thrown off or away,

like hearts on marble, like syllables, like
butchers' discards.

The true story is vicious
and multiple and untrue

after all. Why do you
need it? Don't ever

ask for the true story.

LANDCRAB I

A lie, that we come from water.
The truth is we were born
from stones, dragons, the sea's
teeth, as you testify,
with your crust and jagged scissors.

Hermit, hard socket
for a timid eye,
you're a soft gut scuttling
sideways, a blue skull,
round bone on the prowl.
Wolf of treeroots and gravelly holes,
a mouth on stilts,
the husk of a small demon.

Attack, voracious
eating, and flight:
it's a sound routine
for staying alive on edges.

Then there's the tide, and that dance
you do for the moon
on wet sand, claws raised
to fend off your mate,
your coupling a quick
dry clatter of rocks.
For mammals
with their lobes and tubers,
scruples and warm milk,
you've nothing but contempt.

Here you are, a frozen scowl
targeted in flashlight,
then gone: a piece of what
we are, not all,
my stunted child, my momentary
face in the mirror,
my tiny nightmare.

LANDCRAB II

The sea sucks at its own
edges, in and out with the moon.
Tattered brown fronds
(shredded nylon stockings,
feathers, the remnants of hands)
wash against my skin.

As for the crab, she's climbed
a tree and sticks herself
to the bark with her adroit
spikes; she jerks
her stalked eyes at me, seeing

a meat shadow,
food or a predator.
I smell the pulp
of her body, faint odour
of rotting salt,
as she smells mine,
working those martian palps:

seawater in leather.
I'm a category, a noun
in a language not human,
infra-red in moonlight,
a tidal wave in the air.

Old fingernail, old mother,
I'm up to scant harm
tonight; though you don't care,

you're no-one's metaphor,
you have your own paths
and rituals, frayed snails
and soaked nuts, waterlogged sacks
to pick over, soggy chips and crusts.

The beach is all yours, wordless
and ripe once I'm off it,
wading towards the moored boats
and blue lights of the dock.

ONE MORE GARDEN

In the garden, waxy jasmine
& hibiscus jostle, the chaliceflower
one fat petal, a creamy orifice;
the punky stems
bulge visibly into fruit,
drop and are picked & sucked;
sex grows on trees, I told you.

Bananaquit, a squeal,
fingernail on blackboard,
at noon predictable,

and at dusk
slight pillowsmell of mildew,
the waterdrop of secret
green throats, their clear notes.

On bare feet, fishbelly
white, I wince
over stubble & around
sheepshit, to hang the wash.

The walls crack & sprout
ants & airy
lizards, varnish
peels off the ceiling, the sea is as blue
every morning as it always
was. In the salt air, hot
as tears, things manmade split & erode
as usual, but faster.

I should throw my gold watch
into the ocean and become
timeless. I'd stand more chance
here as a gourd, making
more gourds, as a belly
making more. Kiss your
thin icon goodbye, sink memory
& hope. Join the round
round dance. Fuck the future.

POSTCARD

I'm thinking about you. What else can I say?
The palm trees on the reverse
are a delusion; so is the pink sand.
What we have are the usual
fractured coke bottles and the smell
of backed-up drains, too sweet,
like a mango on the verge
of rot, which we have also.
The air clear sweat, mosquitoes
& their tracks; birds, blue & elusive.

Time comes in waves here, a sickness, one
day after the other rolling on;
I move up, it's called
awake, then down into the uneasy
nights but never
forward. The roosters crow
for hours before dawn, and a prodded
child howls & howls
on the pocked road to school.
In the hold with the baggage
there are two prisoners,

their heads shaved by bayonets, & ten crates
of queasy chicks. Each spring
there's a race of cripples, from the store
to the church. This is the sort of junk
I carry with me; and a clipping
about democracy from the local paper.

Outside the window
they're building the damn hotel,
nail by nail, someone's
crumbling dream. A universe that includes you
can't be all bad, but
does it? At this distance
you're a mirage, a glossy image
fixed in the posture
of the last time I saw you.
Turn you over, there's the place
for the address. Wish you were
here. Love comes
in waves like the ocean, a sickness which goes on
& on, a hollow cave
in the head, filling & pounding, a kicked ear.

LATE NIGHT

Late night and rain wakes me, a downpour,
wind thrashing in the leaves, huge
ears, huge feathers,
like some chased animal, a giant
dog or wild boar. Thunder & shivering
windows; from the tin roof
the rush of water.

I lie askew under the net,
tangled in damp cloth, salt in my hair.
When this clears there will be fireflies
& stars, brighter than anywhere,
which I could contemplate at times
of panic. Lightyears, think of it.

Screw poetry, it's you I want,
your taste, rain
on you, mouth on your skin.

PETIT NEVIS

Salt water scours out
the head, fills it with salt
water, blue to the
horizon, which tilts this way and that

and levels again at a shore
like this one. A jetty, sandflies.
This is the shed where they drag
the whales each year, here's where they cut them up
with implements from two centuries
ago, and the hook and cauldron
where they boil them down.

Sometimes there's a bone
left over, on the beach
over the ridge, porous and burned
white. Seagrapes, dry scrub
bent by the wind, a surf

that grinds everything smaller:
here's a braincoral
shrunk to a nugget, a boulder
from an old volcano knucklesized now,
the colour of dried blood.

Where is it you belong
in all this blue and bleached
green? Under the noon sun, which glares
on everything with equal
blindness. Here
on the sand anything human

is extra. You're extra,
a mistake, something found:
a gift, a contradiction.

I've been away from you
too long for comfort, not long enough
for safety. Safety would be
this island, a charred
bone, an ocean, a red stone.

HOTEL

I wake in darkness
in a strange room.

There's a voice on the ceiling
with a message for me.

It repeats over & over
the same absence of words,

the sound love makes
when it's been run to earth,

forced into a body,
cornered. Upstairs there's a woman

with no face and an unknown
animal shuddering in her.

She bares her teeth and whimpers;
the voice ripples through walls & floor,

released now, freed & running
downhill to the sea like water.

It tests the air here and finds
space. It enters

me and becomes mine.

DINNER

Dining room: tinsel festoons,
gold stars, hibiscus grown from plastic.
This is an island where everything
that's eaten comes by plane
in crates, except the fish
whose gills and bladders litter the beach.

Here's where we trudge
from one meal to the next,
feeding on starch and grease.
Engorged buttocks and
thighs jiggle by,
surly soft paunches.
Sugar etches the teeth.

Offshore, breakers mark the reef
and its growths, knees and bristles,
nibbled vertebrae, lost bottles,
beaks and rubbery mouths.

The tapedeck groans about love,
also imported, the sea
groans about nothing
the glassy faces leaning
down into it can hear.
It's a shadow, purple
in the halflight, spined and menacing.
I love you, whines the soprano.

It's the same song, and mine is
also. Why sneer at those ancient
rhythms, constant and constantly
broken, our cut feet move to? Unless you need
nothing. That whisper
and thud is the undertow
of all this filagree · heartbeat · the same
desire and greed.

NOTHING

Nothing like love to put blood
back in the language,
the difference between the beach and its
discrete rocks & shards, a hard
cuneiform, and the tender cursive
of waves; bone & liquid fishegg, desert
& saltmarsh, a green push
out of death. The vowels plump
again like lips or soaked fingers, and the fingers
themselves move around these
softening pebbles as around skin. The sky's
not vacant and over there but close
against your eyes, molten, so near
you can taste it. It tastes of
salt. What touches
you is what you touch.

SMALL POEMS FOR
THE WINTER SOLSTICE

1

A clean page: what
shines in you is not nothing,
though equally clear & blue

and I'm old enough to know
I ought to give up wanting
to touch that shining.

What shines anyway?
Stars, cut glass, and water,
and you in your serene blue shirt

standing beside a window
while it rains, nothing
much going on, intangible.

*

To put your hand
into the light reveals
the hand but the light also:
shining is where they touch.

Other things made of light:
hallucinations & angels.
If I reach my hands
into you, will you vanish?

2

Free fall
is falling but at least it's
free. I don't even know
whether I jumped or was pushed,
but it hardly matters now
I'm up here. No wings
or net but for an instant
anyway there's a great
view: the sea,
a line of surf, brown cliffs
tufted with scrub, your upturned
face a white zero.
I wish I knew
whether you'll catch or watch.

3

Mouth to mouth
I'm bringing you back to life.
Why did you drown like that
without telling?
What numbed you? What
rose over your head
was gradual and only
everybody's air,
standard & killing.
Your head floats on your hand,
on water, you turn
over, your heart returns
unsteadily to its two strong notes.
I'm bringing you back
to life, it's mutual.

4

Towards my chill house in this sloppy weather,
hands on the cold wheel, hoping there'll be a fire;
slush on the glass, past an accident,
then another. Somewhere there's one more,
mine. In a minuet we just
miss each other, in an accident
we don't. Dance is intentional but
did you miss me or
not, was it too close
to the bone for you, was that
pain, am I gone? Nothing's
broken, nevertheless I'm skinless,
the gentlest touch would gut me.
Slowly, slowly, nobody wants a mess.
I float over the black roads, pure ice.

5

No way clear,
I write on the lines across this yellow
paper. Poetry. It's details
like this that drag
at me, and the nasty little bells
on the corners I pass on my way
to meet you: singing of hunger,
darkness & poverty.

6

The weeks blink out, the winter solstice
with its killed pine branches
and tiny desperate fires
is almost upon us

again & again, in fifty versions:
the trees turn dull blue, the fields dun

for the last time.
We have a minute, maybe two

in which we're walking together
towards the edge of that evergreen forest
we'll never enter

through the drifted snow
which is no colour,
which has just fallen,

which has just fallen,
on which we will leave no footprints

7

This poem is mournful
& sentimental and filled
with complaints: where were you?
When I needed you.

I'd like to make
a bouquet of nice clean words for you,
hand it to you and walk away,
function accomplished. I can't
do it. This is the shortest day
of the year, shrunken,
blueveined & cold, deafmute.
That's me on the corner, sleet
down my neck, wordless. Where are you?

8

You think I live in a glass tower
where the phone doesn't ring
and nobody eats? But it does, they do
and leave the crumbs & greasy knives.

In the front room dogsmells
filter through the door,
dirty fur coats & the insides
of carnivore throats. Neglect
& disarray, cold ashes drift
from the woodstove onto the floor.
Cats with their melting spines festoon
themselves in every empty
corner. Who's fed them? Who knows?

What I want you to see
is the banality of all this, even
while I write the doorbell
pounds down there, constant assaults
of the radio, one more
blameless crushed face, another
pair of boots drips in the hall.

There's no mystery, I want to tell
you, none at all, no more
than in anything else. What I do
is ordinary, no
surprise, like you
no trickier than sunrise.

9

Some would say there's no excuse
for this collusion: while men
kill & mutilate each other, call it politics, burn
buildings & children, skewer
women through the eyes or bellies, we
hold hands in corner bars.

A distraction, takes your mind
off work or the jerky screen
where death is an event, love
isn't, unless it's double
suicide. How can I justify
this gentle poem then in the face of sheer
horror? A genteel pretence,
stupidity in this place of cracked
grey mud where the babies bloat
& wither and there's only one
quick exit from starvation.

Holding hands is a luxury
indulged in by the fat.
Still, if there were nothing
but killing or being killed then why not
kill? I know you by your
opposites. I know your absence.

10

Of course I'm a teller
of mundane lies, such as: I'll try
never to lie to you. Such as:
the day after today the earth will
tilt on its axis towards the sun
again, the light will turn stronger,
it will be spring and you'll
be happy. Such as:
I can fly. I wish I could believe
it. Instead I'm stuck
here, in this waste of particulars,
truths, facts. Teeth, gloves & socks.
I don't trust love
because it's no shape or colour.

11

I'd like you to be surprised
though, and greedy as a child
who does not need choices because all
choices are possible, and simple
as candy. A handful
of balloons, a grab and suddenly
you're in midair. Pure
delight, that's what you ought
to have, no difficult
chains & nets on your hands,
no tangled futures.

See, I hold out my hands to you,
lineless as if they'd been scalded,
wiped out. What innocence. Suppose I could do this,
would you want me to?

12

Afternoon: a wreck of paper
& coloured ribbons.
It rains & rains. You're as absent
as if unborn. Family swarms round us,
the machines hum:
clean dishes & music, dinner, steam
on the windows. What are you
up to? The same
things, I assume. The same dream.
Today you're the blank
side of the moon.

There's a cooked bird, a sharp knife:
that's real
and to be dealt with.

Arrogance, for me
to believe I know you
or anything about your life.

13

I'm in your hands, you say, meaning
something quite different: a way
of passing choice. Nevertheless
you're what I got handed,
not wanting it, like those cards
printed with the finger alphabet
the deaf & dumb nail you with in bus
stations. An embarrassment, but more
than that: some object
made of glass, lucid & simple
and without a name or known
function. I can learn you
by touch & guesswork
or not. Meanwhile I hold you
in my hands, true, wondering what
to make of you and what you'll make
of me. A gesture
of the hands, clear
as water. The letter A.

14

Is this really your fate,
to enter poetry and become transparent?

No ground under you, no feet or shoes,
no carpets, breadcrusts, calendars, no buttons,
pockets, hair, fur on the body, blood, unless
I put them there?

You're no good to me as a rumour,
blank & timeless. The year
isn't a clear circle or some
dream of a clock but one shadowy
moment after the next.
There's no choice, I have to take you
with all the clutter,
the fears, justified
or not, the smoky furniture,
dubious flesh, fatigue, the nagging
of daily voices, your obscure heart
neither of us can see, which beats
softly under my hand,
flying in darkness. Let's believe
you know your way.

1

When I knew them they were an ordinary couple, she
smiled and laughed a lot, she was a physiotherapist I
think, and there was nothing wrong with him either,
that you could see, except he was a little, you know.
That summer they went on their vacation together,
they always went on their vacation together, to Spain,
that was back when you could still afford it, and
everyone thinks he cut her up and left her in four
garbage cans around the city, or maybe not in cans,
do they have cans there? In Barcelona, except it
wasn't Barcelona. It's like that guy who was keeping
his wife in the freezer, you know? And a couple of
kids went looking for some popsicles or whatever.
He didn't even have a lock on the freezer, some
people are pretty dumb. He said they'd gone to
Madrid, except it wasn't Madrid, and one day she just
went out for a walk and never came back, but the
landlady, in Barcelona or whatever it was, says she
saw him back at the flat or whatever it was they'd
rented, after the day he said they'd gone to wherever.
And the cans with her in them were in Barcelona, not
Madrid. So they're there and he's here and naturally
they want him to go over, for questioning they say,
and naturally he won't. He says he doesn't need the
distress all over again. I'll bet. Not that I would either
if I was him. I saw him in the supermarket last week.
He was holding an eggplant and he said, *Aubergine*,
it's a much better word, don't you think? He was
running his fingers over the purple skin. He hasn't
changed a bit.

2

A long time ago I was desperately in love. Desperately is what I mean, in fact you could leave out the love and still get a good picture. He felt the same way and the strange thing was, neither of us could understand a word the other said. Because of this we used to throw dishes at one another, to attract each other's attention I suppose; we used to shout. For some reason they were always his dishes. Once I ran into his kitchen and cut a hole in my arm with his kitchen scissors, not a very big hole, so he could see there was real blood inside, but he didn't understand that either. It isn't sex that's the problem, it's language. Or maybe love makes you deaf, not blind, because now we go out to dinner every once in a while and we can understand each other perfectly, we tell jokes and we laugh at them, we really think they're funny. I look at him and I can't believe we once threw dishes at each other, but we did. I can remember which plates, which cups, which glasses, and which ones broke.

3

My friend called me on the telephone and said, I'm
going to kill myself. Why? I said. He's left me, **she**
said. I have nothing to live for. All right, I said, **how**
are you going to do it? Pills? No, she said, that would
make me sick. If it doesn't work, I mean. I can't stand
having my stomach pumped out, it's humiliating.
Well, a gun then, I said. Think of the mess, she said.
It's indelible, and I hate loud noises. Hanging, I said.
You look so awful, she said. You could say the same
of drowning, I said. Well, I guess that's that, she said,
but what am I going to do, now that he's left me and I
have nothing to live for? Who told you it has to be for
anything? I said. But were you living for him when he
was there? No, she said. I was living in spite of him, I
was living against him. Then you should say, I have
nothing to live against, I said. It's the same thing, isn't
it? she said. I said No.

4

Most people in that country don't eat eggs, she told me, they can't afford to; if they're lucky enough to have a chicken that lays eggs they sell the eggs. There is no such thing as *inside*, there's no such thing as *I*. The landscape is continuous, it flows through whatever passes for houses there, dried mud in and out, famine in and out, there is only *we*. That's why they can kill so many of us and not make any difference. To make a difference they would have to kill all of us. They cut off the hands and heads to prevent identification but they cannot prevent it. Everyone knows who has been shot and thrown into the sea, who has been beaten, which man or woman has been methodically raped, which left to starve and burn in a pit under the noon sun. It's bright there and clear, you can see a long way.

As for my lover, she told me, we had to separate. None of us can afford to live with just one other. You get careless, you forget how much you want to live, you start making bargains with yourself, you become dangerous to others. That kind of love is a weapon they can use against you. Among those of us who still have heads and hands there are no marriages.

5

I don't think about you as much as I ought to; I don't have to, you're there whether I think about you or not. Many people aren't.

When I do think about you it's not what you'd expect. I don't want to be with you: most of the time that would be an interruption, for both of us. I like to consider you going about your routine. I think about you getting up, brushing your teeth, having breakfast. I vary the breakfasts, though I don't devise anything too fanciful for you, I stick to cornflakes, orange juice, eggs, things like that. No strawberries out of season. I find it soothing to think about you eating these mundane and in fact somewhat austere breakfasts. It makes me feel safe.

But why should you go on eating breakfast at the same time, in the same way, day after day, just so I will be able to feel safe? You're contented enough, true, but there must be more. I'm getting around to that. One of these mornings, when you reach the bottom of your cup, coffee or tea, it could be either, you will look and there will be a severed finger, bloodless, anonymous, a little signal of death sent to you from the foreign country where they grow such things. Or you will glance down at your egg, four minutes, sitting in its dish white and as yet uncracked and serene as ever, and sunlight will be coming out of it. But on second thought your coffee cup will be vacant and the egg, when you finally close your eyes and slice it open blindly with the edge of your spoon, will have nothing in it that is not ordinarily there. Then you will know that at last I have imagined you perfectly.

NOTES TOWARDS A POEM
THAT CAN NEVER BE WRITTEN

A CONVERSATION

The man walks on the southern beach
with sunglasses and a casual shirt
and two beautiful women.
He's a maker of machines
for pulling out toenails,
sending electric shocks
through brains or genitals.
He doesn't test or witness,
he only sells. My dear lady,
he says, You don't know
those people. There's nothing
else they understand. What could I do?
she said. Why was he at that party?

FLYING INSIDE YOUR OWN BODY

Your lungs fill & spread themselves,
wings of pink blood, and your bones
empty themselves and become hollow.
When you breathe in you'll lift like a balloon
and your heart is light too & huge,
beating with pure joy, pure helium.
The sun's white winds blow through you,
there's nothing above you,
you see the earth now as an oval jewel,
radiant & seablue with love.

It's only in dreams you can do this.
Waking, your heart is a shaken fist,
a fine dust clogs the air you breathe in;
the sun's a hot copper weight pressing straight
down on the thick pink rind of your skull.
It's always the moment just before gunshot.
You try & try to rise but you cannot.

THE ARREST OF THE STOCKBROKER

They broke the hands of the musician
and when despite that he would not stop singing
they shot him. That was expected.

You expected the poet hung upside down
by one foot with clothesline: in your head
you coloured his hair green. Art needs martyrs.

And the union leader with electrodes
clipped to the more florid
parts of his body, wired like
an odd zoological diagram:
if you don't keep your mouth shut
they'll choose the noise
you emit. Anyone knows that.
In some way he wanted it.

Reading the papers, you've seen it all:
the device for tearing out fingernails,
the motors, the accessories,
what can be done with the common pin.
Not to mention the wives and children.

Who needs these stories
that exist in the white spaces
at the edges of the page,
banal and without shape, like snow?

You flip to the travel ads; you're unable
to shake the concept of tragedy,
that what one gets
is what's deserved, more
or less; that there's a plot,
and innocence is merely
not to act.

Then suddenly you're in there,
in this mistake, this stage, this box,
this war grinding across
your body. You can't believe it.

Not only that, he's in here with you,
the man with the documents,
the forms, the stamps, the ritual prayers, the seals,
red & silver, and the keys, the signatures.

Those are his screams you hear,
the man you were counting on
to declare you legitimate:
the man you were always counting on
to get you out.

TORTURE

What goes on in the pauses
of this conversation?
Which is about free will
and politics and the need for passion.

Just this: I think of the woman
they did not kill.
Instead they sewed her face
shut, closed her mouth
to a hole the size of a straw,
and put her back on the streets,
a mute symbol.

It doesn't matter where
this was done or why or whether
by one side or the other;
such things are done as soon
as there are sides

and I don't know if good men
living crisp lives exist
because of this woman or in spite
of her.
        But power
like this is not abstract, it's not concerned
with politics and free will, it's beyond slogans

and as for passion, this
is its intricate denial,
the knife that cuts lovers
out of your flesh like tumours,
leaving you breastless
and without a name,
flattened, bloodless, even your voice
cauterized by too much pain,

a flayed body untangled
string by string and hung
to the wall, an agonized banner
displayed for the same reason
flags are.

FRENCH COLONIAL

For Son Mitchell

This was a plantation once,
owned by a Frenchman. The well survives,
filled now with algae, heartcoloured
dragonflies, thin simmer of mosquitoes.

Here is an archway, grown over
with the gross roots of trees,
here's a barred window,
a barn or prison.
Fungus blackens the walls
as if they're burned, but no need:
thickening vines lick over
and through them, a slow
green fire. Sugar,
it was then. Now there are rows
of yellowing limes, the burrows
of night crabs. Five hundred yards
away, seared women in flowered dresses
heap plates at the buffet.
We'll soon join them.
The names of the bays:
Hope, Friendship and Industry.

The well is a stone hole
opening out of darkness,
drowned history. Who knows
what's down there? How many
spent lives, killed muscles.
It's the threshold of an unbuilt
house. We sit on the rim
in the sun, talking
of politics. You could still
drink the water.

A WOMEN'S ISSUE

The woman in the spiked device
that locks around the waist and between
the legs, with holes in it like a tea strainer
is Exhibit A.

The woman in black with a net window
to see through and a four-inch
wooden peg jammed up
between her legs so she can't be raped
is Exhibit B.

Exhibit C is the young girl
dragged into the bush by the midwives
and made to sing while they scrape the flesh
from between her legs, then tie her thighs
till she scabs over and is called healed.
Now she can be married.
For each childbirth they'll cut her
open, then sew her up.
Men like tight women.
The ones that die are carefully buried.

The next exhibit lies flat on her back
while eighty men a night
move through her, ten an hour.
She looks at the ceiling, listens
to the door open and close.
A bell keeps ringing.
Nobody knows how she got here.

You'll notice that what they have in common
is between the legs. Is this
why wars are fought?
Enemy territory, no man's
land, to be entered furtively,
fenced, owned but never surely,
scene of these desperate forays
at midnight, captures
and sticky murders, doctors' rubber gloves
greasy with blood, flesh made inert, the surge
of your own uneasy power.

This is no museum.
Who invented the word *love*?

CHRISTMAS CAROLS

Children do not always mean
hope. To some they mean despair.
This woman with her hair cut off
so she could not hang herself
threw herself from a rooftop, thirty
times raped & pregnant by the enemy
who did this to her. This one had her pelvis
broken by hammers so the child
could be extracted. Then she was thrown away,
useless, a ripped sack. This one
punctured herself with kitchen skewers
and bled to death on a greasy
oilcloth table, rather than bear
again and past the limit. There
is a limit, though who knows
when it may come? Nineteenth-century
ditches are littered with small wax corpses
dropped there in terror. A plane
swoops too low over the fox farm

and the mother eats her young. This too
is Nature. Think twice then
before you worship turned furrows, or pay
lip service to some full belly
or other, or single out one girl to play
the magic mother, in blue
& white, up on that pedestal,
perfect & intact, distinct
from those who aren't. Which means
everyone else. It's a matter
of food & available blood. If mother-
hood is sacred, put
your money where your mouth is. Only
then can you expect the coming
down to the wrecked & shimmering earth
of that miracle you sing
about, the day
when every child is a holy birth.

TRAINRIDE, VIENNA-BONN

i

It's those helmets we remember,
the shape of a splayed cranium,
and the faces under them,
ruthless & uniform

But these sit on the train
clean & sane, in their neutral
beige & cream: this girl smiles,
she wears a plastic butterfly, and the waiter gives
a purple egg to my child
for fun. Kindness abounds.

ii

Outside the windows the trees flow
past in a tender mist,
lightgreen & moist with buds

What I see though is the black trunks,
a detail from Breughel:
the backs of three men returning
from the hunt, their hounds following,
stark lines against the snow.

iii

The forest is no darker
than any forests, my own
included, the fields we pass
could be my fields; except
for what the eye puts there.

In this field there is a man
running, and three others, chasing,
their brown coats
flapping against their boots.

Among the tree roots the running man
stumbles and is thrown
face down and stays there.

iv

What holds me
in the story we've all heard
so many times before:

the few who resisted,
who did not do what they were told.

This is the old fear:
not what can be done to you
but what you might do
yourself, or fail to.

This is the old torture.

v

Three men in dark archaic
coats, their backs to me, returning
home to food and a good fire,
joking together, their hounds following.

This forest is alien
to me, closer than skin,
unknown, something early
as caves and buried, hard,

a chipped stone knife, the
long bone lying in darkness
inside my right arm: not
innocent but latent.

SPELLING

My daughter plays on the floor
with plastic letters,
red, blue & hard yellow,
learning how to spell,
spelling,
how to make spells

*

and I wonder how many women
denied themselves daughters,
closed themselves in rooms,
drew the curtains
so they could mainline words.

*

A child is not a poem,
a poem is not a child.
There is no either/or.
However.

*

I return to the story
of the woman caught in the war
& in labour, her thighs tied
together by the enemy
so she could not give birth.

Ancestress: the burning witch,
her mouth covered by leather
to strangle words.

A word after a word
after a word is power.

*

At the point where language falls away
from the hot bones, at the point
where the rock breaks open and darkness
flows out of it like blood, at
the melting point of granite
when the bones know
they are hollow & the word
splits & doubles & speaks
the truth & the body
itself becomes a mouth.

This is a metaphor.

*

How do you learn to spell?
Blood, sky & the sun,
your own name first,
your first naming, your first name,
your first word.

NOTES TOWARDS A POEM
THAT CAN NEVER BE WRITTEN

For Carolyn Forché

i

This is the place
you would rather not know about,
this is the place that will inhabit you,
this is the place you cannot imagine,
this is the place that will finally defeat you

where the word *why* shrivels and empties
itself. This is famine.

ii

There is no poem you can write
about it, the sandpits
where so many were buried
& unearthed, the unendurable
pain still traced on their skins.

This did not happen last year
or forty years ago but last week.
This has been happening,
this happens.

We make wreaths of adjectives for them,
we count them like beads,
we turn them into statistics & litanies
and into poems like this one.

Nothing works.
They remain what they are.

iii

The woman lies on the wet cement floor
under the unending light,
needle marks on her arms put there
to kill the brain
and wonders why she is dying.

She is dying because she said.
She is dying for the sake of the word.
It is her body, silent
and fingerless, writing this poem.

iv

It resembles an operation
but it is not one

nor despite the spread legs, grunts
& blood, is it a birth.

Partly it's a job,
partly it's a display of skill
like a concerto.

It can be done badly
or well, they tell themselves.

Partly it's an art.

v

The facts of this world seen clearly
are seen through tears;
why tell me then
there is something wrong with my eyes?

To see clearly and without flinching,
without turning away,
this is agony, the eyes taped open
two inches from the sun.

What is it you see then?
Is it a bad dream, a hallucination?
Is it a vision?
What is it you hear?

The razor across the eyeball
is a detail from an old film.
It is also a truth.
Witness is what you must bear.

vi

In this country you can say what you like
because no one will listen to you anyway,
it's safe enough, in this country you can try to write
the poem that can never be written,
the poem that invents
nothing and excuses nothing,
because you invent and excuse yourself each day.

Elsewhere, this poem is not invention.
Elsewhere, this poem takes courage.
Elsewhere, this poem must be written
because the poets are already dead.

Elsewhere, this poem must be written
as if you are already dead,
as if nothing more can be done
or said to save you.

Elsewhere you must write this poem
because there is nothing more to do.

VULTURES

Hung there in the thermal
whiteout of noon, dark ash
in the chimney's updraft, turning
slowly like a thumb pressed down
on target; indolent V's; flies, until they drop.

Then they're hyenas, raucous
around the kill, flapping their black
umbrellas, the feathered red-eyed widows
whose pot bodies violate mourning,
the snigger at funerals,
the burp at the wake.

They cluster, like beetles
laying their eggs on carrion,
gluttonous for a space, a little
territory of murder: food
and children.

Frowzy old saint, bald-
headed and musty, scrawny-
necked recluse on your pillar
of blazing air which is not
heaven: what do you make
of death, which you do not
cause, which you eat daily?

I make life, which is a prayer.
I make clean bones.
I make a grey zinc noise
which to me is a song.

Well, heart, out of all this
carnage, could you do better?

LAST POEM

Tonight words fall away from me like shed clothing
thrown casually on the floor as if there's no
tomorrow, and there's no tomorrow.

One day halfway up the mountain or down the freeway,
air in any case whistling by,
you stop climbing or driving and know you will never get there.

I lie on a blue sofa and suck icecubes
while my friends and the friends of my friends and women
I hardly know get cancer.
There's one a week, one a minute; we all discuss it.

I'm a plague worker, I brush finger to finger,
hoping it's not catching, wondering how to say
goodbye gracefully and not merely snivel.
There are small mercies, granted, but not many.

Meanwhile I sit here futureless with you:
in one second something will wrench like a string or a zipper
or time will slide on itself like the granite sides of a fissure
and houses, chairs, lovers collapse in a long tremor.

That's your hand sticking out of the rubble.
I touch it, you're still living;
to have this happen I would give anything,
to keep you alive with me despite the wreckage.

I hold this hand as if waiting for the rescue
and that one action shines like pure luck.
Because there's nothing more I can do I do nothing.

What we're talking about is a table and two glasses,
two hands, a candle, and outside the curtained window
a charred landscape with the buildings and trees still smouldering.
Each poem is my last and so is this one.

EARTH

It isn't winter that brings it
out, my cowardice,
but the thickening summer I wallow in
right now, stinking of lilacs, green
with worms & stamens duplicating themselves
each one the same

I squat among rows of seeds & imposters
and snout my hand into the juicy dirt:
charred chicken bones, rusted nails,
dogbones, stones, stove ashes.
Down there is another hand, yours, hopeless,
down there is a future

in which you're a white white picture
with a name I forgot to write
underneath, and no date,

in which you're a suit
hanging with its stubs of sleeves
in a cupboard in a house
in a city I've never entered,

a missed beat in space
which nevertheless unrolls itself
as usual. As usual:
that's why I don't want to go on with this.

(I'll want to make a hole in the earth
the size of an implosion, a leaf, a dwarf
star, a cave
in time that opens back & back into
absolute darkness and at last
into a small pale moon of light
the size of a hand,
I'll want to call you out of the grave
in the form of anything at all)

USE

What do I want
you for? If there's an
answer it's nothing, you're
of no use in my life, a
pure indulgence. What
would I want a picture
on the wall for? To look
at, but why? All such
questions end in stillness; yet I
want you too
much, I want
also to use you, I want you
to be used & to glisten
with it, like hot muscle or metal
against stone or a shape
of wood caressed

by years of hands, to some
purpose. If I'm to be
burned slowly cell by
cell or worn down that's
how. Of what use is the body
dancing, except to mark
the vacancy against which we
measure sound? Close your
eyes, out of sight is out of
time, draw your hand
again & again over my
skin & watch me vanish
into darkness, flicker
and reappear, this is my use for
you, shine with it, give
out light

SUNSET I

This is a different beach,
grudging & thin. Behind, the standard
industrial detritus. In front the generous
gasping sea, which flops against the shore
like a stranded flounder.
Tonight there's no crescendo
in the sun either, no brilliant red
catastrophes, no slashed
jugulars; merely a smudged egg.

We walk in our boots, too chilled
for skin on the sand, which is anyway
smeared with grease and littered
with exhausted lunches and clumps of torn-out
hair. There's a seagull,
avarice in its yellow
eye. It would like us face down
in the ebbtide. I hold your hand, which probably
detaches at the wrist. Heat theory states
I'll soon be as cold as you. Plato
has a lot to answer for.

I'd take you where
I'm going, but you won't come,
you're snowbound & numb & neatly
ordered. No remedy, drop everything,
wade into the illegal
greying sea, with its dirty
sacred water and its taste of dissolving metal,
which is nearly dead but still trying,
which is not ethical.

VARIATIONS ON THE WORD *LOVE*

This is a word we use to plug
holes with. It's the right size for those warm
blanks in speech, for those red heart-
shaped vacancies on the page that look nothing
like real hearts. Add lace
and you can sell
it. We insert it also in the one empty
space on the printed form
that comes with no instructions. There are whole
magazines with not much in them
but the word *love*, you can
rub it all over your body and you
can cook with it too. How do we know
it isn't what goes on at the cool
debaucheries of slugs under damp
pieces of cardboard? As for the weed-
seedlings nosing their tough snouts up
among the lettuces, they shout it.
Love! Love! sing the soldiers, raising
their glittering knives in salute.

Then there's the two
of us. This word
is far too short for us, it has only
four letters, too sparse
to fill those deep bare
vacuums between the stars
that press on us with their deafness.
It's not love we don't wish
to fall into, but that fear.
This word is not enough but it will
have to do. It's a single
vowel in this metallic
silence, a mouth that says
O again and again in wonder
and pain, a breath, a finger-
grip on a cliffside. You can
hold on or let go.

SUNSET II

Sunset, now that we're finally in it
is not what we thought.

Did you expect this violet black
soft edge to outer space, fragile as blown ash
and shuddering like oil, or the reddish
orange that flows into
your lungs and through your fingers?
The waves smooth mouthpink light
over your eyes, fold after fold.
This is the sun you breathe in,
pale blue. Did you
expect it to be this warm?

One more goodbye,
sentimental as they all are.
The far west recedes from us
like a mauve postcard of itself
and dissolves into the sea.

Now there's a moon,
an irony. We walk
north towards no home,
joined at the hand.

I'll love you forever,
I can't stop time.

This is you on my skin somewhere
in the form of sand.

VARIATION ON THE WORD *SLEEP*

I would like to watch you sleeping,
which may not happen.
I would like to watch you,
sleeping. I would like to sleep
with you, to enter
your sleep as its smooth dark wave
slides over my head

and walk with you through that lucent
wavering forest of bluegreen leaves
with its watery sun & three moons
towards the cave where you must descend,
towards your worst fear

I would like to give you the silver
branch, the small white flower, the one
word that will protect you
from the grief at the center
of your dream, from the grief
at the center. I would like to follow
you up the long stairway
again & become
the boat that would row you back

carefully, a flame
in two cupped hands
to where your body lies
beside me, and you enter
it as easily as breathing in

I would like to be the air
that inhabits you for a moment
only. I would like to be that unnoticed
& that necessary.

RAIN

It rains & rains & the trees
light up like stones underwater:
a haze of dull orange,
a yellow mist,
on the ground a purple kelp
of shed leaves.

The branches send out their tentacles:
catkins & red tufts
groping for summer.

From the window I can see
the meadow I walked through yesterday,
spiney mosses
in last year's papery grass, white flowers
tiny & chilly.

Here is a room
where you will never be;
outside, a road
where you will never
be with me. It's
hard to believe.

This is not a season
but a pause
between one future & another,
a day after a day,
a breathing space before death,
a breathing, the rain

throwing itself down out of the
bluegrey sky, clear joy.

MUSHROOMS

i

In this moist season,
mist on the lake and thunder
afternoons in the distance

they ooze up through the earth
during the night,
like bubbles, like tiny
bright red balloons
filling with water;
a sound below sound, the thumbs of rubber
gloves turned softly inside out.

In the mornings, there is the leafmould
starred with nipples,
with cool white fishgills,
leathery purple brains,
fist-sized suns dulled to the colour of embers,
poisonous moons, pale yellow.

ii

Where do they come from?

For each thunderstorm that travels
overhead there's another storm
that moves parallel in the ground.
Struck lightning is where they meet.

Underfoot there's a cloud of rootlets,
shed hairs or a bundle of loose threads
blown slowly through the midsoil.
These are their flowers, these fingers
reaching through darkness to the sky,
these eyeblinks
that burst and powder the air with spores.

iii

They feed in shade, on halfleaves
as they return to water,
on slowly melting logs,
deadwood. They glow
in the dark sometimes. They taste
of rotten meat or cloves
or cooking steak or bruised
lips or new snow.

iv

It isn't only
for food I hunt them
but for the hunt and because
they smell of death and the waxy
skins of the newborn,
flesh into earth into flesh.

Here is the handful
of shadow I have brought back to you:
this decay, this hope, this mouth-
ful of dirt, this poetry.

OUT

This is all you go with,
not much, a plastic bag
with a zipper, a bar of soap,
a command, blood in the sink,
the body's word.

You spiral out there,
locked & single
and on your way at last,
the rings of Saturn brilliant
as pain, your dark craft
nosing its way through stars.
You've been gone now
how many years?

Hot metal hurtles over your eyes,
razors the flesh, recedes;
this is the universe
too, this burnt view.

Deepfreeze in blankets; tubes feed you,
your hurt cells glow & tick;
when the time comes you will wake
naked and mended, on earth again, to find
the rest of us changed and older.

Meanwhile your body
hums you to sleep, you cruise
among the nebulae, ice glass
on the bedside table,
the shining pitcher, your white cloth feet
which blaze with reflected light
against the harsh black shadow
behind the door.

Hush, say the hands
of the nurses, drawing the blinds
down   hush
says your drifting blood,
cool stardust.

BLUEJAYS

While you lie, staked out
on that white oblong, scarcely choosing
to breathe, hooked up
to life by one clear thread,

the jays come & go, still eat
the seeds you left there,
scatter them on the lawn among
the pears & limp apples.

Who tore that hole in you?
The birds fly in the white air,
their cries slicing the frozen
space between tree & tree,
piercing blue, angels

or needles. It was you,
some voice that said
the only way is through,

some angel that wanted you
to choose · to breathe.

Brighteyed and razor-
billed, without
apologies, the birds devour
anything that will feed
their quick lives:

        your sunflowers.

Next summer
something forgotten will bloom there.

DAMSIDE

This used to be a dam;
now everything thrown
in washes over, continuous
and shining like hair.

The children scramble on the rim.
For them it's something for fishing
in and spitting into.
They trail barbed hooks in the water,
jigging for some doomed mouth.

We walk downstream
and up again. Pinecones and the first green
antennae spiralling through the stubble
by the pathside, wet breadcrusts
and greasy rubbish
that the just-born flies revel in.

The river's brown
and not something you'd drink
unless you thought you were dying.

If this were a poem I'd trust the river,
kneel and cup my hands
around its liquid ice, its ozone-
blue. If this were a poem you'd live forever.

As it is, I can offer you
only this poor weather:
my chilled hands, the fragments
of a noon in early spring,
an east wind which includes
both of us, and the stained river,
a prayer, a sewer, a prayer.

BLUE DWARFS

Tree burial, you tell me, that's
the way. Not up in but under.
Rootlets & insects, you say as we careen
along the highway with the news on
through a wind thickening with hayfever.
Last time it was fire.

It's a problem, what to do
with yourself after you're dead.
Then there's before.

The scabby wild plums fall from the tree
as I climb it, branches & leaves
peeling off under my bootsoles.
They vanish into the bone-coloured
grass & mauve asters
or lie among the rocks and the stench

of woodchucks, bursting & puckered
and oozing juice & sweet pits & yellow
pulp but still
burning, cool and blue
as the cores of the old stars
that shrivel out there in multiples
of zero. Pinpoint mouths
burrowing in them. I pick up the good ones
which won't last long either.

If there's a tree for you it should be
this one. Here
it is, your six-quart basket
of blue light, sticky
and fading but more than
still edible. Time smears
our hands all right, we lick it off, a windfall.

HIGH SUMMER

High summer,
our lives here winding down.

Why are we building fences?
There's nothing we can keep out.

Wild mustard, hornworms, cutworms
push at the edges of this space

it's taken eight years to clear.
The fields, lush green and desolate

as promises, are still pretending
to be owned. Nothing

is owned, not even the graves
across the road with the names

so squarely marked.
Goodbye, we credit

the apple trees, dead
and alive, with saying.

They say no such thing.

LAST DAY

This is the last day of the last week.
It's June, the evenings touching
our skins like plush, milkweed sweetening
the sticky air which pulses
with moths, their powdery wings and velvet
tongues. In the dusk, nighthawks and the fluting
voices from the pond, its edges
webbed with spawn. Everything
leans into the pulpy moon.

In the mornings the hens
make egg after egg, warty-shelled
and perfect; the henhouse floor
packed with old shit and winter straw
trembles with flies, green and silver.

Who wants to leave it, who wants it
to end, water moving
against water, skin
against skin? We wade
through moist sun-
light towards nothing, which is oval

and full. This egg
in my hand is our last meal,
you break it open and the sky
turns orange again and the sun rises
again and this is the last day again.